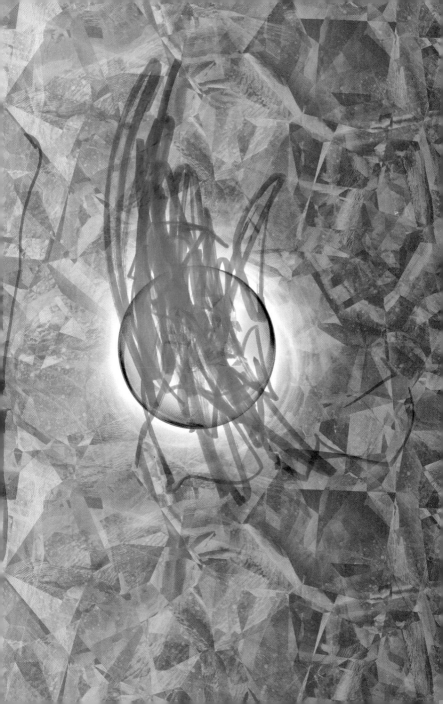

FIRE AND ICE

Scholastic Inc.

"The Long Climb," "Fear of Fire," and "Operation Nap Time" written by Greg Farshtey.

Illustrated by Ameet Studio

No part of this publication may be reproduced, stored in a retrieval system, or transmitted in any form or by any means, electronic, mechanical, photocopying, recording, or otherwise, without written permission of the publisher. For information regarding permission, write to Scholastic Inc., Attention: Permissions Department, 557 Broadway, New York, NY 10012.

ISBN 978-0-545-69526-8

LEGO, the LEGO logo, the Brick and Knob configurations, the Minifigure and LEGENDS OF CHIMA are trademarks of the LEGO Group. ©2014 The LEGO Group. Produced by Scholastic Inc. under license from the LEGO Group.

Published by Scholastic Inc. SCHOLASTIC and associated logos are trademarks and/or registered trademarks of Scholastic Inc.

10 9 8 7 6 5 4 3 2 1   14 15 16 17 18 19/0

Printed in the U.S.A.   40

First Scholastic printing, September 2014

MIX
Paper from
responsible sources
FSC® C020056

TABLE OF CONTENTS

CHIMA . . . ON ICE!

Deep in the underground caverns of Chima, an ancient race of Ice Age warriors called the Hunters lay frozen for thousands of years. No one in Chima even knew they existed . . . until now. These vicious warriors have awoken from their centuries-long sleep, and they want to freeze all of Chima!

My name is Laval, and I'm the Prince of the Lion Tribe. Not long ago, the tribes of Chima were united in a fight against the evil Scorpions, Spiders, and Bats in the Outlands. Together, we defeated them. But the Hunters are powerful enemies, unlike anything we've ever faced before.

The Hunters began marching through our land, turning everyone and everything in their path into ice. Their first attack froze the entire Crocodile Swamp. Cragger barely escaped. But his parents, King Crominus and Queen Crunket, were frozen. We quickly realized the tribes of Chima must unite once again to face this new enemy.

THE HUNTERS

There are three main Hunter Tribes: the Saber Tooth Tigers, the Mammoths, and the Vultures.

The Saber Tooth Tigers are the most aggressive Hunters. They don't care who they attack—just as long as they are attacking someone. Under the strict command of their leader, Sir Fangar, the Saber Tooth Tigers will never back down from a fight.

The Mammoths are the largest and strongest of the Hunters, but they are not very aggressive. They'd be happy living quietly on the frozen plains. If provoked, however, Mammoths become extremely ferocious.

The Vultures are a cunning tribe, but they're also lazy. They are experts at laying traps because it's often the easiest way to accomplish their tasks. The Vultures would rather wait for an enemy to wear himself out in a snare than waste energy fighting him.

All of the Hunters are able to freeze anything upon touch. They have decayed a bit over the millennia spent in the ice. But despite their zombie-like appearance, their ability to freeze upon contact is as strong as ever. Even our CHI-powered weapons are useless against these new enemies.

SIR FANGAR

This ferocious Saber Tooth Tiger leads the Hunters in their conquest. In an odd way, he feels he has the soul of an artist and that it is his right to "reshape" Chima's image with his freezing touch.

Sir Fangar gained this inflated view of himself while attending one of the Grand Institutions of Learning run by the Phoenix Tribe thousands of years ago. The Phoenixes intended to civilize the wilder side of Chima back then. Unfortunately, Sir Fangar used all his skills and wisdom for evil, attempting to freeze Chima into submission. The Phoenix Tribe stopped him, but now that Sir Fangar has awoken, he's determined to not let anything stand in his way.

When a Hunter freezes a tribe member, they remain alive but trapped inside the block of ice. Sir Fangar likes to keep his frozen opponents as "trophies" of his victories. His ultimate dream is to freeze a Phoenix as revenge for when they defeated the Hunters so long ago.

LAVAL SAYS . . .

"Sir" Fangar isn't actually a knight. He just insists everyone call him "Sir" as a sign of respect.

DREAMS ABOUT FIRE

When the Hunters attacked Chima, Eris began having strange dreams about catching on fire. She was worried, because the dreams felt very real. In them, she also saw the Lion and Crocodile vehicles catching fire, and Mount Cavora, too. She thought that her dreams might be visions of the future, but nobody believed her—not even me, Laval, her best friend.

In one dream, Eris saw a fiery temple. She realized the temple was on top of Mount Cavora and that she needed to go there.

At first, we couldn't believe what Eris wanted to do. An impenetrable force field surrounds Mount Cavora. No one had ever successfully passed through it before! But during a fierce battle against the Vultures, Eris tricked them into freezing one of Mount Cavora's waterfalls. After that, she convinced me and Cragger to climb up the frozen waterfall with her.

We knew it was going to be a very risky mission. The chances for success were slim. But we had to give it a try for our friend. And for Chima.

THE PHOENIX CITY

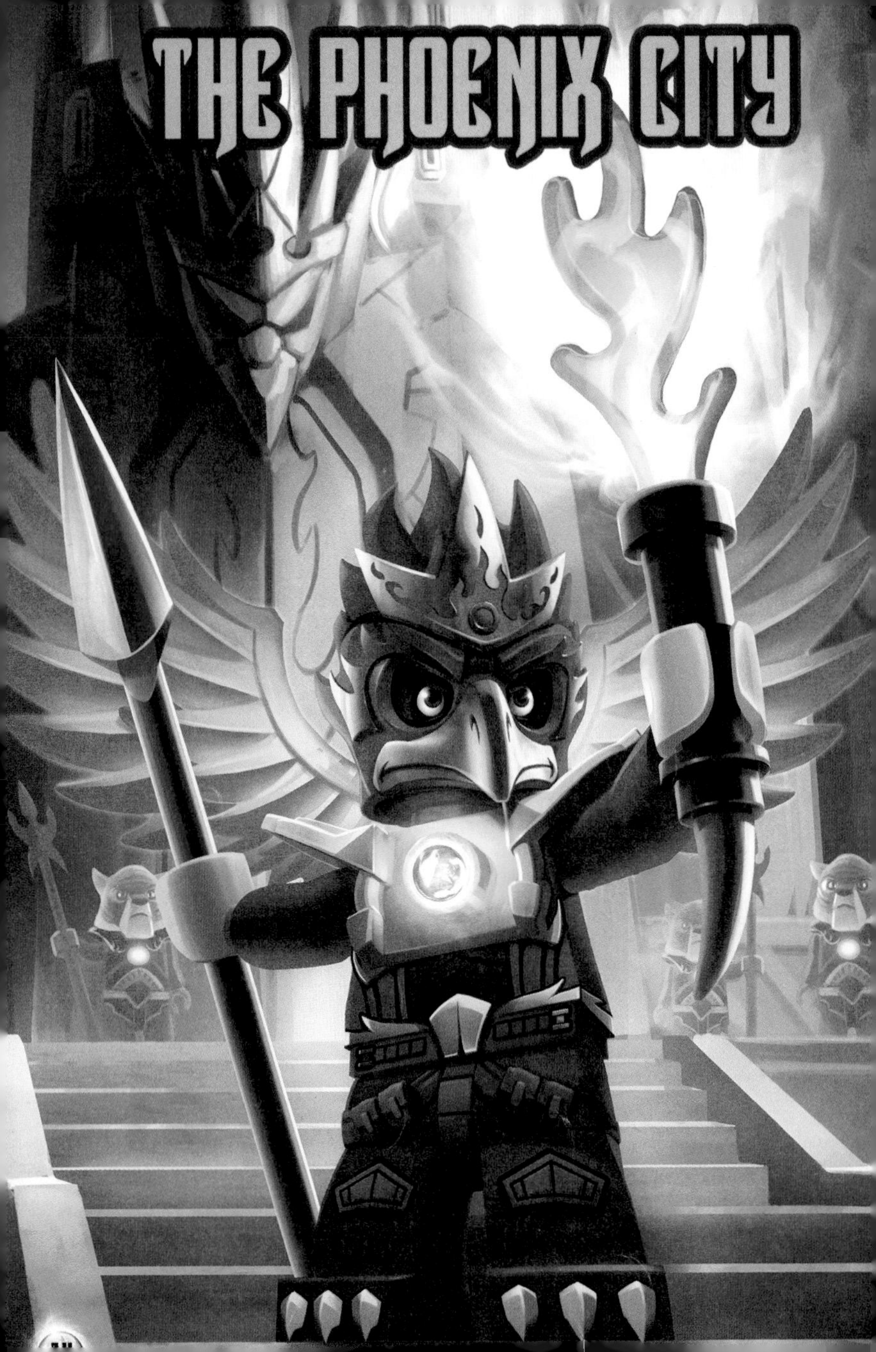

Climbing the frozen waterfall of Mount Cavora was the craziest and most dangerous thing that Eris, Cragger, and I have ever done. But we were very lucky—it was the only way to get inside the floating mountain.

When we finally got there, we couldn't believe our eyes. A marvelous city was hidden on top of Mount Cavora beneath rocks and jungle. Everything seemed magical: There were stairways to nowhere, backward-flowing fountains, and upside-down-growing plants. Most amazingly, the walls of the entire city were coated in thin veils of flame. Despite all that fire, the residents—the ancient Phoenix Tribe—were able to walk through the city without getting burned. And at the very top of the city was the Phoenix Temple. The fiery temple from Eris's vision.

We learned from the Phoenixes that this wasn't the first time the Hunters had tried to conquer Chima. In ancient times, Sir Fangar had led them on a mission to freeze the land and everything in it. It was the Phoenix Tribe who stopped them, and we realized that only the Phoenixes could give us a weapon powerful enough to defeat these enemies once more.

FIRE CHI

The Phoenixes introduced us to Fire CHI, the only kind of CHI that can counter a Hunter's freezing attacks.

When plugged into a warrior's harness, Fire CHI provides a new kind of CHI-Up. Its power boost is much stronger than a traditional CHI Orb, and it is accompanied by a flaming Power Warrior Glow. This warm glow protects a warrior from being frozen when in battle.

Although it is hot, Fire CHI does not burn the warrior using it. Rather, its powers extend through the warrior's harness and to their weapons as well. Swords deliver flaming strikes. Cannons shoot fiery beams. And explosive weapons burst with enough heat to melt any kind of frozen obstacle.

When an orb of Fire CHI is placed into a warrior's vehicle, it instantly transforms into a powerful Fire Vehicle. Filled with the power of the Fire CHI, vehicles literally expand into larger versions of themselves and become faster and more dangerous.

With Fire CHI, we can fight the Hunters on equal terms. Now there is a real hope we can save Chima!

TURN THE PAGE FOR
THREE FIRE-POWERED LEGENDS OF
CHIMA™
STORIES!

"**H**old on!" yelled Laval.

"No kidding!" growled Cragger. "Got any other original ideas?"

Some fifty feet below, Eris gasped. Cragger was dangling by one hand from an icy ledge, his feet swinging wildly in the air. Up above, Laval was reaching down to grab the Crocodile, but couldn't quite make it. If Cragger lost his grip, it would be a long fall to the ground below.

"Laval, can you reach him?" Eris cried.

"I think so—just wait there, Cragger," Laval shouted. "I'll climb down to you."

"Where am I going to go?" Cragger answered, yelling to be heard over the howl of the wind. "It's hang on here or be a Croc pancake!"

Eris couldn't believe how quickly everything had gone wrong. Chima was facing a crisis: Icy creatures called Hunters had rampaged across the land, freezing everything in their path. Right around the time that the Hunters showed up, she had also begun having strange dreams. No, not dreams . . . they were more like visions.

In them, Eris kept seeing flashes of Mount Cavora on fire. And past the flames, burning bright in the center, was a shining temple on top of the mountain. Somehow, Eris

just knew that if they could reach the top of the mystical mountain, hidden inside was an answer that would help them save all of Chima.

But Mount Cavora floated high in the air. In order to reach it, Eris had tricked one of the Hunter Tribes, the Vultures, into freezing the waterfalls. Now, she and her friends were trying to reach the top of the mountain by climbing the frozen waterfalls that stretched from the ground up to the face of the rock.

At first, Laval and Cragger hadn't believed her. But the battle against the Hunters was going poorly. Cragger's parents had been frozen solid, and more and more tribe members were falling victim to the ice daily. Laval and Cragger realized that Eris's dreams might actually be a vision of how to save Chima. So they had agreed to make the climb with her. Now they were halfway up to the top. The question was, could they make it any farther?

"I'm on my way!" Eris shouted. "My wings are half-frozen. I can't fly! But I'm climbing as fast as I can."

"I'll wave to you on my way down," Cragger yelled back. "Can somebody help me out here? Crocs do mud and swamps and swimming and diving. But ice climbing? Not so much."

"Well, I do have one idea," Eris shouted up. "But it's really dangerous."

"Dangerous for who?" asked Cragger.

"Well . . . all of us."

"On a scale of one to ten, how dangerous are we talking about?" asked the Crocodile.

"Umm . . . fifteen," Eris answered.

"Thanks, but I think I'll pass," said Cragger. "I got myself into this, I'll get myself out . . . somehow."

Eris shook her head. "You've said that before, Cragger. Remember?"

Cragger did indeed remember. It was many years ago, on a similar climb the three of them had made together, when they were much younger . . .

"I know this is important," said Cragger. "But remind me why I am doing it with you two?"

Laval glanced at the Croc. He had known Cragger since they were both little, but he had never really gotten to be too friendly with the Crocodile.

As for Eris, Laval barely knew her at all. Yet here they were, about to scale a peak together. They were each on the verge of becoming full-fledged warriors in their tribes. But first . . . the mountain.

It had no name. Somehow, the mountain seemed too powerful and too great a symbol to have a random title attached to it. For as long as anyone could remember, climbing it was a ritual every young member of every tribe carried out. Reaching the top meant you were ready for anything your tribe might ask of you in the future.

The "rules" of the climb said that you should do it with members of other tribes, but preferably not ones you were already friends with. The point of the journey was to learn to work with others, even if they were strangers. That's how a Lion, an Eagle, and a Crocodile came to be making their treks on the same day.

"Save your breath for climbing," Laval said to Cragger. "We won't need the rope or the spikes on the lower part of the peak, but it gets a lot steeper as we get higher up."

"And the last one up is a skunk's uncle," Cragger said, grinning.

Eris rolled her eyes. "Wow, you're so mature . . . *not.*"

The Crocodile flashed his sharp teeth at her. "That's what I don't like about Eagles. They always have their

beaks in the air . . . along with everything else."

"Come on, you two," Laval said in as commanding a voice as he could. "Are we going or not?"

Like Laval had said, the early part of their climb was easy. The base of the mountain was a gentle slope that wound this way and that. Laval tried to make small talk with Eris, but she seemed to be a little shy. The one subject she did chatter away on was mountains and some of the dangers about them.

"I've flown over lots and lots of peaks," she explained. "So I've seen all kinds of mountain paths. Winding ones, rocky ones, steep ones, even one that was basically a flowing river—"

"Give me a swamp any day," Cragger interrupted. "You always know where you stand in a swamp."

"Yeah." Laval laughed. "In the mud."

A short while later, the climb began to get tougher. Of the three, Laval was the best at scrambling up the slopes, but even he struggled at times. When they were about halfway up, they came to a part of the mountain that was so steep it seemed impossible to climb.

"There's a ledge way up there," Eris pointed out. "If we could reach that, we could keep going."

"Well, you can fly up to it, right?" asked Laval.

Eris shook her head. "No. The rules say you have to climb. No using wings."

"All right," said Cragger. "You guys give me a boost and I'll pull you up. I'm the strongest, after all."

"Ha!" said Laval. "You're not stronger than me! Why don't you give me a boost?"

"I'll give you a boost, all right . . ." growled Cragger.

"Um, are we going to stand here all day while you two argue?" asked Eris. "Tell you what, I'll pick. Cragger, you go first."

The Crocodile smiled broadly as he stepped on the shoulders of the Eagle and Lion to get up to the ledge. Laval glared at Eris. "What's the big idea?" he whispered.

"If you want him to be part of the team, you have to let him be a hero sometimes," whispered Eris. "Lions aren't the only ones with pride, you know."

Once atop the ledge, Cragger leaned over and grabbed Eris's hand. He pulled her up beside him. Then the two of them helped Laval up as well.

"See? Nothing to it," Cragger said. "There's nothing a Croc can't do when he puts his mind to it."

Laval started to say something, then glanced at Eris and changed his mind. He wasn't happy with the decision she had made, but he thought he understood it, at least a little. He decided she was pretty smart, for someone who wasn't a Lion.

They kept climbing. Cragger seemed to be really enjoying himself now, telling tales of life in the swamp.

Beneath his rough manner, it seemed like Cragger really did want to be friends. Eris wondered if Crocodiles just assumed others didn't like them, so they acted unpleasant to keep everyone away. Once they felt accepted, they warmed up. Eris had to admit Cragger's stories were funny. Even Laval laughed a few times.

Now they were three-quarters of the way to the peak. They still had plenty of hours of daylight left. Eris figured they would be able to make it all the way up and back down and still be home for supper.

Then she heard the noise.

At first, she thought it was thunder. But there weren't any clouds in the sky. Then, as the rumbling grew louder and the ground started to shake, she realized with a sinking feeling exactly what it was.

"Rockslide!" she yelled.

Laval and Cragger looked up and gasped. It seemed like half the mountain was sliding down toward them! They were too high up to leap out of the way, and there was no place to take cover.

"Oh, no!" shouted Cragger.

Laval thought fast. "There's just one chance, but you're going to have to trust me—both of you!"

Cragger hesitated. Crocodiles were raised to take care of themselves and not rely on help from outsiders. It was a hard habit to break. "I'll get out of this on my own!" he said.

"No. You won't," Laval said firmly, grabbing the Croc with one hand and Eris with the other.

What followed was a display of skill, speed, and luck like neither Cragger nor Eris had ever seen before. Laval leaped into the air, pulling them along with him. He landed on one of the rocks tumbling down the mountain. Quickly, he jumped from rock to rock, not only surfing the rockslide—but surfing it up the mountain! At any moment, a misstep or a badly timed leap could have meant disaster. But Laval somehow managed to keep going, guiding his companions to safety.

When the rockslide was finally over, the three found themselves almost at the peak. They had survived the climb and the incredible danger as well.

"Wow," said Cragger. "I have to admit, that was . . . amazing."

"Told you," gasped Laval, out of breath. "You just had to trust me. I know what I'm doing . . . most of the time," he added, with a smile.

"Yeah, well . . . okay," said Cragger.

"I sure will!" said Eris, grinning.

A lot has happened since then, Eris thought as she struggled to climb up to where Cragger was still dangling from the icy ledge. *But one thing's the same—we have to trust one another if we're going to make it through this!*

"I can't climb down to him," Laval yelled above the gusting wind. "The ice is too slippery. And I can't reach him from here!"

"Yes, you can," said Eris. "Loop the rope around your feet, Laval, and hang upside down."

"I knew it," said Cragger. "She's crazy."

Laval looked uncertain. "Are you sure about this, Eris?"

"Trust me!" Eris replied.

Laval did as Eris asked, first securing his feet with the rope to a thick, sturdy icicle, and then flipping over so that his back was against the ice wall. He reached down and grabbed Cragger's free hand. "I've got him, but I can't pull him up like this!"

"Now comes the hard part," said Eris. "Cragger, you have to let go of your handhold on the ice!"

"What?!" exclaimed Cragger. "I'm not letting go of anything!"

"Trust me!" yelled Eris. "It's the only way!"

Reluctantly, Cragger let go of the icy ledge he had been clinging to. Laval grunted, struggling to hold onto his friend now that he was supporting the Crocodile's full weight.

"Now, Laval—" Eris began.

"I know what to do!" said the Lion. "You just be ready!"

Laval began to swing back and forth, relying on the rope to keep him secured to the ice. Like a pendulum, he swung Cragger to the right and left, building up momentum with each pass. He went higher and higher with each swing, until Cragger was actually above Laval.

"Now, Cragger!" yelled the Lion. "Let go and grab the rope!"

Cragger waited until he was as high as Laval could swing him. Then he let go of his friend and leaped for the rope. He managed to catch it with one hand. But below him, the rope had slipped from Laval's feet—the Lion was falling!

"Hang on, Laval!" Eris cried. She sprang off the side of the ice and caught Laval in midair, her wings struggling to keep the two of them aloft. Just before they were going to tumble out of the sky, she banked back toward the ice. Laval was able to grab onto the rope and to her, but couldn't manage to get a foothold on the ice. He could feel his hand starting to slip.

The next thing Laval knew, a strong grip had seized his wrist. He looked up to see Cragger smiling. "Come on," said the Crocodile. "We can't do this without you, fur-face."

With Cragger's help, Laval and Eris climbed back securely onto the ice. Laval clapped a hand on Cragger's shoulder. "Yeah, you're pretty good to have around, too, scale-head."

Eris sighed. "Some things never change," she said. "And am I glad of that!"

FEAR OF FIRE

t was evening in Chima. Light from the campfire flickered across Laval's face as he and his friends mapped out their latest strategy to battle the Hunters. It was a good plan: use Fire CHI to scatter the Saber Tooth Tigers and Mammoths into smaller groups. That way, it would be easier to defend against them.

There was just one problem.

"I said no," snarled Worriz. "Do you need me to spell it? N-O."

Laval sighed. It was the fifth plan using Fire CHI that Worriz had shot down.

"So, what's your great idea?" snapped Cragger. "Growl at them? Yeah, that will send the Hunters running."

"Hey, my Wolf Pack can scare anyone off!" Worriz replied hotly.

"Sure, 'cause no one wants to catch your fleas," snorted Cragger.

"Guys!" Laval cut in. "We're supposed to be planning an attack on the Hunters, not fighting with each other—so knock it off!"

"Oh, I've had enough," grumbled Cragger, getting to his feet. "Every time we try to map out a strategy, old fur-and-claws here says no."

"Maybe Worriz has a good reason," Eris said.

Everyone looked at the Wolf, waiting for him to explain. But Worriz's only response was "Count me out, and the Wolves with me." Then he rose and walked away.

"He's chicken," said Cragger. "We should just go ahead without him and his pack."

It was hard not to think that Cragger was right. What other reason could there be for Worriz's behavior? Now that the tribes had the Fire CHI, they had a real chance to defeat the Hunters. But Worriz didn't seem to want to attack.

"Wolves are known for many things, my friend," said Razar. "But fear is not one of them."

"Well, something is bothering him," said Laval, standing up. "And I am going to find out what it is."

"Do you need our help?" asked Eris.

Laval shook his head. "I think I'd better handle this by myself, pride leader to pack leader."

Laval followed Worriz all the way back to where the Wolf Pack had made camp. He found the Wolves pacing restlessly. Laval decided to stay downwind so the Pack wouldn't pick up his scent just yet. The night breeze carried their conversations to where Laval hid behind a bush.

"When are we going to fight?"

"What's all this sitting around for?"

"Are we Wolves or not?"

"You know, if you are going to spy on us, you might make a little less noise on your approach."

Laval jumped. That voice had come from behind him. It belonged to Windra, the white Wolf. She smiled menacingly.

"I was just . . . well . . . yes, I was eavesdropping," said Laval. "I needed to know—"

"Why the Wolves won't fight the way you want us to?" Windra finished for him. "Come with me."

Laval followed Windra quietly around the pack's makeshift camp. Well away from where the Wolves were talking, Windra showed Laval a pile of Fire CHI. It looked like the Wolf Tribe had never used any of the Fire CHI they had been given by the Phoenix Tribe.

"It's the only weapon powerful enough to defeat the Hunters," said Windra, "but Worriz won't let us use it. He won't even tell us why. Now that you know, maybe you can change his mind."

The next day, Laval took Worriz aside. "We have something to do."

"What?" grumbled the Wolf.

"Eris was just on a scouting mission. She spotted some Saber Tooth Tigers on the move. It looked like they were going to attack the Wolf Pack camp from the east. If we move fast, we can cut them off."

"Just the two of us?" Worriz asked. "Not that I mind getting my paws dirty, but two against Tigers seems a little nuts."

"Don't worry. We have this," Laval said, producing an orb of Fire CHI.

Worriz looked like he had smelled something bad. "Not for me, thanks."

"Then I'll use it," said Laval. "Let's go."

The two warriors slipped out of camp. They moved as quietly as they could through the forest, watching for Hunters or any other threat. After a while, Laval spotted what he had come for: a huge pile of ice blocks across the forest path.

"I thought I heard something behind us," said the Lion. "I'm going to go check it out. Here, you use the Fire CHI to melt that ice barrier."

Worriz frowned. "Why can't we just climb over it?"

"We don't have time," Laval replied. "Just melt it!"

Laval ran off, leaving Worriz holding the Fire CHI as far away from his body as he could. The Lion was sure Worriz would use the CHI if he thought the safety of his tribe was at stake. And after that, all the Wolves would be able to use it. There weren't actually any Saber Tooths anywhere around—it was all just a trick. A pretty clever one, Laval thought.

I'll just go around that bend and that will be far enough. Then I'll turn back, thought the Lion. He jogged around a patch of trees . . . and found himself staring right at four Saber Tooth Tigers! Their eyes widened at the sight of him and fierce smiles crossed their lips. Laval made a U-turn and ran as fast as he could back toward Worriz.

The Wolf was still looking back and forth between the Fire CHI and the ice blocks when Laval returned.

"Go! Move! Run!" yelled Laval. "Saber Tooths!"

Worriz started scrambling up the pile of ice. "I thought you said they were coming from the east."

"Those were made-up Tigers," Laval said, climbing rapidly up the barrier. "These are real!"

They made it to the top and didn't take time to look back. They half climbed, half slid down the other side. "We need to lead them away from our camps," said Laval.

"There's high ground just ahead," said Worriz. "Maybe we can hold them off from there. It's just past the river."

Laval suddenly slowed. "The river?"

"Yeah. What are you waiting for?"

"Me and water . . . don't get along," said Laval. "I really, *really* don't like it."

"You mean like I don't like Fire CHI?" Worriz sneered. "I really don't like it, either. But you keep trying to make me use it."

Behind them, the Saber Tooths had reached the top of the ice barrier.

"We'd better move," said Laval. "Find a place where one of us can CHI up."

"It'll be you," said Worriz. "Fire and I don't get along."

"I don't get it," Laval cried as they ran. "Wolves use torches and campfires all the time."

"That's different!" Worriz leapt over a frozen tree trunk. "This Fire CHI is real power, blasting out from your hands and roasting everything around you. I . . . I don't know if I can control it."

They had reached the riverbank now. The partially frozen water flowed just quickly enough to make Laval shudder. He looked over his shoulder. The Tigers were gaining.

"All right, listen. We need to lead them to the high ground away from our camps so we can fend them off. I'm going to swim across the river even if it terrifies me, because I have to. I'm not going to let down my tribe. And once we're on the other side, I'll use the Fire CHI and drive the tigers off."

Without another word, Laval plunged into the icy water. Worriz was surprised to find himself actually feeling real respect for the Lion. But with Saber Tooths breathing down his neck, there was no time to get all warm and fuzzy. Worriz followed him in.

The half-frozen water swirled around them.

"Come on," Laval gasped, shivering in the freezing cold. "We're almost there—"

Suddenly, a chunk of ice snagged Laval's cape and dragged him down! In a splash, the Lion disappeared beneath the swirling ice and waves!

Worriz swam hard to the spot where the Lion had sunk and dove under. He reached blindly, his lungs burning from the strain of holding his breath. Finally, he felt Laval's mane. He grabbed a furry fistful and pulled as hard as he could. Laval popped up over the surface, coughing and sputtering.

Together, they made it to the other side of the river. But Laval was exhausted and shivering badly.

"Use the CHI!" Laval gasped. "I can't do it now. Use it or the Tigers will get us both—and maybe our tribes, too!"

Worriz looked hard at Laval, and then at the Tigers, who were already halfway across the river. Then he shut his eyes and plugged the CHI Orb into his harness.

Instantly, he felt a fiery surge of energy filling his whole body. He had the power, but more than that, he was in control of it.

The Wolf opened his eyes and snarled at the Tigers. "Oh, are you boys going to be sorry."

Unleashing his new energy, Worriz created a wall of flame in front of the Saber Tooths. They immediately backed off.

"What's the matter?" yelled Worriz. "Not afraid of a little fire, are you?"

Without waiting for an answer, the Wolf helped Laval to his feet and the two ran off as fast as they could back to the camps.

Later that night, Worriz came up to Laval by the campfire. "Wolves don't say thank you, so that's not what I'm saying," he said. "Okay, maybe you helped me out back there . . . a little . . . but this isn't a thank you."

"Okay," said Laval, grinning.

"I just have one question," Worriz said. "Did you really run into trouble in that river? Or was that just another way to get me to use the Fire CHI?"

"Oh, that." Laval chuckled. "I don't know if I could have made it across on my own or not. But I do know one thing: I'm glad I was able to count on you when it mattered the most."

OPERATION NAP TIME

"**F**all back to the woods!" yelled Eris.

Eagle Warriors looped and zigzagged in the sky, avoiding icy blasts of freezing power from the Vultures. They couldn't believe what was happening. This morning, the Vultures had used a false message from Laval to lure most of the Eagles out the Spire. Once they were gone, the vicious creatures had launched an attack on the Eagles' home!

Eris had led a squadron of her tribe's finest warriors against them, and for a while, it looked like they might be able to hold the Hunters back. But more Vultures kept coming, and all too quickly they surrounded Eagle Spire, preventing the Eagles from being able to get inside. Worse, all the Eagles' Fire CHI was in the Spire. Without it, there was simply no way to defeat the Vultures.

One by one, Eris had watched as her friends were frozen solid in large blocks of ice. Now there was no choice but to retreat.

In the safety of the forest, Eris and the remaining Eagle Warriors discussed battle strategies. "We have to get back into the Spire and secure the Fire CHI," said Eris. "But how?"

Just then, Razar the Raven fluttered down from the sky. He landed next to Eris. "You're going about this the wrong way, my friend."

"What do you mean?" asked Eris.

"I've been keeping an eye on things . . . both eyes, actually. You're never going to beat those guys in a battle. They're too tough." Razar winked. "You need to outthink them. What do they want? What do they need? How can you use that against them? Think like a Raven, Eris!"

Eris tried, but found she could only think like an Eagle. "Do you have a plan?" she asked.

"Do I have a plan?" Razar said, smiling. "I'm a Raven. I was born with a plan. And you can find out all about it . . . for a small fee."

Several promises of trinkets and treasures later, Razar agreed to bring his fellow Ravens back to help defeat the Vultures with his plan. That night, the Ravens returned, each one carrying a bundle. Without making a sound, they snuck up to where some of the Vultures were camped and placed their bundles all around the ground.

The next morning, the Vultures were puzzled to find pillows scattered everywhere.

"Pillows?" asked Eris when she saw what the Ravens had done. "Your plan is pillows?"

"Just wait," replied Razar, chuckling. "It gets better."

The next night, the small Raven strike force came again, this time leaving a pile of crossword puzzles. The night after that, they left a bunch of snacks. (No one was quite sure what Vultures liked to snack on, and no one really wanted to think about it, so they just took a guess.) By the fourth night, the Vultures were sufficiently concerned about new things appearing in their camp every morning that they doubled the guard. It was now too dangerous for even the stealthy Ravens to try to sneak in.

Eris was getting impatient. "All right, it's been three days, and all you have done is furnished the Vultures' playroom," she said to Razar. "How is this getting us closer to the Spire?"

"Remember what I said about figuring out what the enemy wants?" Razar said. "Well, Vultures aren't hard-working like us Ravens. Sure, they'll capture your home and make a big squawk, but they would rather be lying around any day. They just needed an excuse . . . so I gave them one. Look!"

Eris peered at the camp. Most of the Vultures were still on guard, watching for Eagles. But a few were reclining on the pillows, and a few more were eating snacks, and about a half dozen were struggling with a crossword puzzle. She smiled at Razar.

"You mean—?"

"It's like pushing a rock down a hill," the Raven assured her. "It might start out slowly, but it will pick up speed. Have your warriors ready. You'll know when."

Eris kept watch for the next few nights. Pretty soon, she could hear Vultures arguing over who got the softest pillows. Then she could hear the sound of snacks being munched on. Finally, a chorus of snores came from the Vulture camp.

"Let's go," whispered Eris. She and the rest of the Eagle tribe took flight, soaring over the sleeping Vultures. As fast as they could, they swept into the Spire and grabbed the Fire CHI. By the time the Vultures figured out what was happening, it was too late. The Eagles had taken the opportunity to CHI up and they were ready for battle.

The Vultures never knew what hit them. Used to winning every fight, they didn't know what to do when they were on the losing end. They tried to rally, but the Fire CHI power of the Eagles singed their tail feathers and sent them flapping for cover. Eris felt a surge of pride as she saw the Vultures flee. The Spire belonged to the Eagles again!

When the last Vulture was gone, Razar flew up to Eris with a smile.

"Thanks for all your help," Eris said.

"Nothing to it," Razar said, laughing. "If there's one thing I know, it's never underestimate the power of a pillow!"